David's Dinner Party

Tieska Jumbo

T. Jumbo
Be kind. Be brave. Be yourself.

David's Dinner Party

Jumbo House Publishing

ISBN - 978-1-7352009-1-0 (Paperback)

Illustrations by Baba Mustafa

Dedicated to Daniel, David, and Danny for loving me no matter what and keeping me on my toes.

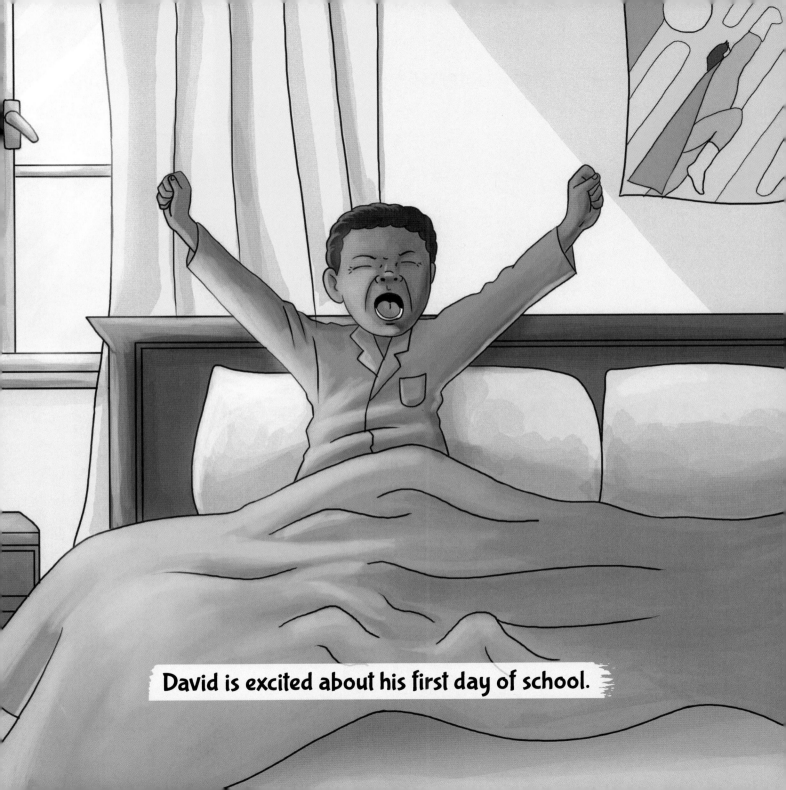

David is excited about his first day of school.

He gets dressed, brushes his teeth, and combs his hair.

David packs his favorite food for lunch, Nigerian Jollof Rice.

In class, David loves answering questions. He feels very smart.

At lunch, David opens his rice. Before he takes a bite, he realizes he's being stared at. David fights back tears. Suddenly, he is no longer hungry.

On the way home, David sits alone on the bus and stares out the window, feeling hungry and sad.

At home, David is still sad. "What's the matter sweetheart?" Mommy asks.

"I'm sorry son. Sometimes, people make fun of what they don't understand. What did you say?"

"Nothing. I just sat there. I almost cried and I didn't want to eat my food anymore. So, I put it away."

"It sounds like you were embarrassed too," says Daddy. "It's okay to feel upset, but we can't let the way other people feel about us change who we are or how we feel about ourselves."

"I know..." mumbles David.

"Ok. What do you want to do?"

David is quiet for a few minutes.

"I want to have a party and invite my classmates.
Then, they can taste it for themselves!"

The next day at school, David is nervous about inviting all his classmates to the party. He doesn't want them to tease him again. But he decides to be brave and invite them all anyway.

On the day of the party, David anxiously walks back and forth afraid nobody will come.

When the doorbell rings, David opens the door to find half his classmates and their parents waiting and smiling.

"You came!" David squeals.

Mommy greets everyone and shows them outside.

"We have a vegetable garden in our backyard. Fresh food gives our meals extra flavor," Mommy says proudly.

"I hope you don't mind, but I could use your help preparing the food today."

The guests agree. Mommy gives every person a task. The children pick the vegetables and the parents chop them.

After finishing their tasks, the families gather around the kitchen table while Mommy explains each step. She lets them taste each of the fresh vegetables before blending and adding them to the stew.

"We use bell peppers in our salads! I love how crunchy they are," says one friend.

"My mommy uses tomatoes to make tomato soup," says another while sniffing the air.

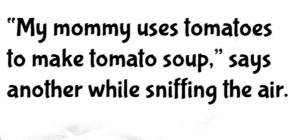

"Why do you have so many bananas?" asks one of the children.

"Those are not bananas, they're plantains," giggles David,

"...and they're so sweet!"

David shows his friends how to slice the plantain. His little brother Danny sprinkles each piece with a tiny bit of salt, so Mommy can fry it.

"All this food smells so yummy. Is it almost done?" asks another child.

Finally, dinner is done and it is time to eat.

David's belly rumbles as he sits down at the table. He takes a bite and smiles. It is still his favorite.

He notices that it is quiet.

He looks up to see everyone else filling their bellies and emptying their plates.

"They like our food!" David thinks to himself.

One by one, the guests sit back, rub their bellies, and thank Mommy for the delicious meal and for sharing their culture.

As the families leave, the kids tell David they will see him at school and the parents ask Mommy for her recipe.

Before going to his room, David turns to Mommy with a big smile and says, "Can you pack my lunchbox with rice for school tomorrow, please?"
"Of course!" says Mommy.

"We're proud of you for being kind to others, while being brave enough to be yourself," says Daddy.

Made in the USA
Columbia, SC
13 August 2020